# Chief Five Heads

by Tracy Turner-Jones and Alex Naidoo

W

Once, there was a man with two daughters.

The elder daughter was proud and lazy.

But the younger daughter was kind.

They lived in a village by a wide river.

Far away, there lived a great chief.

He wanted to get married.

"Would you like to marry the chief?"

the man asked his elder daughter.

"Yes, I would," replied his daughter.

"You must take some friends with you,"

said her father. "It is expected."

"No, I can find my own way,"

said the elder daughter.

3

The next day she set off to the chief's village.

But she soon lost her way.

A little mouse saw that she was lost.

"I'll show you the way," he said.

"I don't need help from a mouse!"

said the girl and she stomped off.

Soon she came across a frog.

"I can show you the way," the frog said.

"I'm marrying a great chief," the girl said.

"I don't need help from a silly frog."

A while later, she met an old woman.

"I'll show you the way," the old woman said.

But the girl said, "I'm too important

to listen to you."

Soon the elder daughter came to
the chief's village.

The chief's sister was getting water
from the river.

"Where are you going?" she asked.

"I am on my way to marry the chief,"
said the elder daughter.

"I will come with you," said the chief's sister.

But the elder daughter walked past her
and on to the village.

The villagers were surprised that she came alone. "The chief will be back later," they said. "You must make food for him."

The mother gave her grain to make bread. The elder daughter saw that the grain was old and dry but mixed it anyway. The bread she made was not good.

That evening, a strong wind blew.

A huge snake slithered into the village.

It had five heads with big round eyes.

The elder daughter didn't know

Chief Five Heads was a snake.

She trembled in fear.

She gave the chief the bread she had made.

It was dry and it tasted horrible.

"I won't marry you," the chief said.

And he sent her home.

So, the younger daughter went to her father.

"May I go to see if the chief will marry me?"

she asked. Her father agreed.

"Now it is my turn to go to the chief,"

she said. I will take a friend with me."

On her way, the younger daughter met

the mouse. "I can show you the way,"

the mouse said.

"Thank you," she replied.

Later, she met the old woman.

"I will show you the way," said the old woman.

The younger daughter gave the old woman some food. Then she went on her way.

Sometime later, the younger daughter
met a rabbit.

"You're nearly at the chief's village,"
the rabbit said. "Be polite to the girl
by the river. And when you're given grain
to make some bread, grind it finely."

The chief's sister was by the river.

"Why are you here?" she asked

the younger daughter.

"I hope to marry the chief,"

the younger daughter said.

"Aren't you scared?" the chief's sister asked.

"No," replied the younger daughter.

So the chief's sister went with them

to the village.

The younger daughter arrived at the village.
The chief's mother gave her grain to make
bread. The younger daughter ground
the grain until it was fine.
Chief Five Heads slithered towards
the younger daughter.

She bravely gave the chief her bread.

It was very tasty.

Chief Five Heads was very happy.

Suddenly he turned into

a handsome young man.

"I was the mouse," he said. "I was also

the rabbit and the old woman. I know you're

good and kind. Please marry me," he said.

And she did.

# Story order

Look at these 5 pictures and captions.
Put the pictures in the right order
to retell the story.

**1**

Chief Five Heads reveals his true
appearance.

**2**

Chief Five Heads rejects the dry bread.

**3**

The elder daughter refuses to listen.

**4**

The younger daughter makes tasty bread.

**5**

The elder daughter wants to leave her village.

# Independent Reading

This series is designed to provide an opportunity for your child to read on their own. These notes are written for you to help your child choose a book and to read it independently.

In school, your child's teacher will often be using reading books which have been banded to support the process of learning to read. Use the book band colour your child is reading in school to help you make a good choice. *Chief Five Heads* is a good choice for children reading at Purple Band in their classroom to read independently.

The aim of independent reading is to read this book with ease, so that your child enjoys the story and relates it to their own experiences.

## About the book

This traditional tale from Africa tells the story of how two sisters both try to marry a chief from another village. The elder sister refuses to listen to the advice of strangers, but the younger sister is more kind. She discovers the true appearence of the chief, and wins his heart.

## Before reading

Help your child to learn how to make good choices by asking: "Why did you choose this book? Why do you think you will enjoy it?" Look at the cover together and ask: "What do you think the story will be about?" Ask your child to think of what they already know about the story context. Then ask your child to read the title aloud. Ask: "What does the title tell you about the snake?" Remind your child that they can sound out the letters to make a word if they get stuck. Decide together whether your child will read the story independently or read it aloud to you.

## During reading

Remind your child of what they know and what they can do independently. If reading aloud, support your child if they hesitate or ask for help by telling the word. If reading to themselves, remind your child that they can come and ask for your help if stuck.

## After reading

Support comprehension by asking your child to tell you about the story. Use the story order puzzle to encourage your child to retell the story in the right sequence, in their own words. The correct sequence can be found on the next page.

Give your child a chance to respond to the story. Ask: "Why did the chief choose the younger daughter to marry? What was different about the younger daughter's behaviour? How would you react to the strangers?"

Help your child think about the messages in the book that go beyond the story and ask: "Why do you think the chief showed his true appearence to the younger daughter?" "Are there tales from other cultures you could compare this to?"

## Extending learning

Help your child predict other possible outcomes of the story by asking: "If the elder daughter had treated the strangers she met more kindly, how do you think the chief would have reacted?"

In the classroom, your child's teacher may be teaching how to use speech marks when characters are speaking. There are many examples in this book that you could look at with your child. Find these together and point out how the end punctuation (comma, full stop, question mark or exclamation mark) comes inside the speech marks. Ask the child to read some examples out loud, adding appropriate expression.

Franklin Watts
First published in Great Britain in 2021
by The Watts Publishing Group

Series Editors: Jackie Hamley and Melanie Palmer
Series Advisors and Development Editors: Dr Sue Bodman and Glen Franklin
Series Designers: Peter Scoulding and Cathryn Gilbert

A CIP catalogue record for this book is
available from the British Library.

ISBN 978 1 4451 7693 2 (hbk)
ISBN 978 1 4451 7695 6 (pbk)
ISBN 978 1 4451 8153 0 (ebook)
ISBN 978 1 4451 7694 9 (library ebook)

Printed in China

Franklin Watts
An imprint of
Hachette Children's Group
Part of The Watts Publishing Group
Carmelite House
50 Victoria Embankment
London EC4Y 0DZ

An Hachette UK Company
www.hachette.co.uk

www.franklinwatts.co.uk

**Answer to Story order: 5, 3, 2, 4, 1**